W9-AJT-098

J
398.2
Sw

$10.99

The sword in the
stone

DATE DUE

FE 17 '89	JUL 03	JY 05 '19
AP 19 '89	UG 05 98	
MY 15 '90	FEB 17 97	
MY 25 '89	MR 18	
JA 3 '91	AL 02	
MR 20 '91	JY 06 '99	
AP 25 '91	JE 17 '13	
JY 30 '91		
JUL 17 '95	JE 7 '02	
FEB 10 3	OC 13 '06	
MR 06 98	JY 27 '16	
APR 11	JY 05 '19	

Eau Claire District Library

DEMCO

THE SWORD
IN THE STONE

Retold by Catherine Storr

Illustrated by Susan Hunter

Raintree Childrens Books
Milwaukee·Toronto·Melbourne·London
Belitha Press Limited·London

79974

Copyright © in this format Belitha Press Ltd., 1985

Text copyright © Catherine Storr 1985

Illustrations copyright © Susan Hunter 1985

Art Director: Treld Bicknell

First published in the United States of America 1985
by Raintree Publishers Inc.
330 East Kilbourn Avenue, Milwaukee, Wisconsin 53202
in association with Belitha Press Ltd., London.

Library of Congress Number 84-18293

Conceived, designed and produced by Belitha Press Ltd.,
2 Beresford Terrace, London N5 2DH

ISBN 0-8172-2113-1 (U.S.A.)

Library of Congress Cataloging in Publication Data

Storr, Catherine.
  The sword in the stone.

  (Raintree stories)
  Summary: A brief retelling of selected parts of the Arthurian legend.
  1. Arthurian romances. [1. Arthur, King. 2. Knights and knighthood—
Fiction. 3. Folklore—England] I. Hunter, Susan, ill. II. Title.
PZ8.1.S882Sw 1985   398.2'2'0942   84-18293
ISBN -8172-2113-1

First published in Great Britain 1985
by Methuen Children's Books Ltd.,
11 New Fetter Lane, London EC4P 4EE

All rights reserved. No part of this book may be reproduced
or utilized in any form or by any means, electronic or
mechanical, including photocopying, recording, or by any
information storage and retrieval system, without permission
in writing from the Publisher.

1 2 3 4 5 6 7 8 9   89 88 87 86 85

Printed in Hong Kong by South China Printing Co.

Note: The story of the legendary King Arthur and his knights is found in
many sources, both French and English. Our story is based on the most
famous of these, *Le Morte d' Arthur, Sir Thomas Malory's Book of King
Arthur and of his Noble Knights of the Round Table* (1469). The
illustrations take their inspiration from Malory and Geoffrey of
Monmouth's *History of the Kings of Britain* (c. 1136) as well as from
Medieval miniature paintings and illuminated manuscripts.

ED.

M any hundreds of years ago, there lived a king called Uther Pendragon. He was King of all England. But he had many enemies who wanted to conquer his kingdom and take it from him. Often, he and his knights had to go into battle.

U ther Pendragon and his wife, Queen Igraine, were to have their first child. Merlin, a magician, said to the King, "You must not keep this child with you in the court. He shall be looked after by your knight, Sir Ector, and his wife. When the baby is born, you must wrap him in cloth of gold and give him to a poor man who will be waiting by your castle gate."

The poor man was really Merlin in disguise. He took the baby far away to Sir Ector. Sir Ector named the baby Arthur, and he and his wife looked after Arthur with their own son, Kay.

Some years later, King Uther Pendragon fell very ill. For three days and nights he could not speak. The barons and knights of his court asked Merlin what they should do. "I shall make him speak," Merlin said.

He came to the King's bedside. "Sir, shall your son, Arthur, be King of all England after you?" he asked.

The King turned to Merlin and said, "Yes. With my blessing. He should claim the crown when I am dead." Then he lay back and died.

Far away in the country, Arthur was growing up. He thought that Sir Ector was his own father and that Kay was his real brother. As the boys grew older they learned all the knightly arts. They were taught to swim and to ride, to fish, and to shoot with the bow and arrow. They learned to wrestle and to fight with staves. They learned to fence and to fight with

swords. They learned to joust in tournaments. They learned hunting and falconry. They learned how to dance and how to speak in knightly fashion to nobles and ladies.

They grew stronger and more clever. Kay was always the stronger, but Arthur was the wiser brother.

At last, one autumn Kay was knighted as Sir Kay.

That winter, Merlin asked the Archbishop of Canterbury to summon all of the nobles and barons and gentlemen in the country to come to London for Christmas. They were to meet in the biggest church in London to pray for a miracle to show them who should be the next King of all England. So the lords came to London for Christmas Day from every part of the country.

EAU CLAIRE DISTRICT LIBRARY

13

On Christmas morning all of the people gathered in the great church to ask God for a sign. When they came out into the churchyard, they saw something that had not been there when they had gone into the church.

It was a great square stone, and in the middle of the stone was stuck a beautiful sword. Written in letters of gold around the stone were these words: "WHOEVER PULLS THIS SWORD OUT OF THIS STONE IS THE RIGHTFUL KING OF ALL ENGLAND."

When all the Christmas prayers
had been said, many nobles and
lords tried to pull the sword out of the
stone. But it stuck fast, and no one
could move it.

"The man who will be able to do this
is not yet here," the archbishop said. He
told ten knights to guard the stone and
the sword night and day, until the New
Year. Then there was a great
tournament, and any man who wished
could try to pull the sword out of the
stone to prove that he was the rightful
king.

O n New Year's day, Sir Ector rode into London to the tournament. With him he brought his own son, Sir Kay, and the young Arthur.

As they neared the tournament, Sir Kay found that he had left his sword at the house in London where they were staying. "Please go back and fetch it for me," Sir Kay said to Arthur.

"Of course I will," Arthur said, and he quickly rode back to their lodgings.

When Arthur arrived at the house, there was no one at home to give him the sword. Everyone had gone to watch the tournament. So Arthur said to himself, "I'll go to the churchyard and take the sword that I saw sticking out of that big stone. Kay can fight with that for today."

He rode back to the churchyard, tied up his horse at the gate, and went in. The ten knights who should have been on guard were away, watching the jousting in the tournament. So Arthur went up to the stone, pulled out the sword, and rode off with it to give to his brother, Sir Kay.

As soon as Sir Kay saw the sword, he knew that it had come from the stone in the churchyard. He ran to find his father and said to him, "Look! Here is the sword out of the stone by the church. I must be the next King of all England."

Sir Ector said, "Let us all three go back to the churchyard together."

When they reached the churchyard, Sir Ector said to Sir Kay, "Swear to me on the Book of Truth how you came by this sword."

"My brother Arthur brought it to me," Sir Kay said.

Sir Ector asked Arthur, "How did you get this sword?"

"I'll tell you," said Arthur. "I went home to get my brother's sword, but there was no one there to give it to me. So I came here, pulled the sword out of the stone, and took it to Kay."

"Let me see if you can put it back again," Sir Ector said.

"That's not difficult," Arthur said, and he put it back into the stone. Sir Ector tried to pull it out again, but he could not.

"Now you try," Sir Ector said to Sir Kay. Sir Kay tried with all his might, but he could not move the sword from the stone.

"Now you," Sir Ector said to Arthur. Again, Arthur pulled it out quickly. Then Sir Ector and Sir Kay knelt down on the ground before Arthur.

But Arthur said, "Why do you kneel to me? You are my own dear father and brother."

"No, my lord Arthur. I am not your true father," Sir Ector said. Then he told Arthur how Merlin had carried him off, as a baby, to be brought up by Sir Ector and his wife as if he were their own son.

Arthur was very sad to know that Sir Ector was not his true father. They went together to the Archbishop and told him how Arthur had pulled the sword from the stone. After Christmas, at Twelfth Night, and again at Candlemas and at Easter, many nobles and lords tried to pull the sword out of the stone. But no one could do it, except Arthur.

There was to be one more trial in the summer, and until then the stone was guarded by ten knights. At the feast of Pentecost, in May, all the nobles and barons and knights gathered again in the churchyard in London. Each man tried with all his might to pull the sword from the stone, for each man wished to be the new King.

But only Arthur could draw out the sword, and he did it easily.

hen all the nobles and the common people cried out, "We will have Arthur for our King. It is God's will."

So Arthur became King of all England, and ruled over the land that his father, King Uther Pendragon, had ruled before him.